It Never, Ever Snows in Florida

written by **Amy Sweezey**

illustrated by Ricardo J. Rodriguez

Bryson –
Thanks for bringing
my book to life!
Amy Sweezey

ABOUT THE AUTHOR

Amy Sweezey is an award-winning Broadcast Meteorologist and mom of three. For more than 20 years, she has delivered daily forecasts on television and spoken to countless groups of children about weather. In "It Never, Ever Snows in Florida," Amy combines her experience with weather, kids, and living in both the cold, snowy Midwest and warm, sunny Florida, to create a fun, educational story for children everywhere. Amy lives in the Orlando area with her family, where it's mostly sunny and hardly ever snows.

Find Amy at http://amysweezey.com.

Book Cover and Interior Design Services by Self-Pub Book Design
www.selfpubbookdesign.com

Illustrations by Ricardo J. Rodriguez
Ricardogalaxy94@gmail.com

ISBN: 978-1-516-80002-5

DEDICATION

To Jaelyn, Anderson & Graycen;
my three amazing, Orlando-born kids who have never, ever seen snow in Florida.

AJ lives in Florida.

Florida is called the "Sunshine State."

Even in the wintertime,

Florida is mostly sunny and mostly warm.

AJ likes to go to
the beach, and run
barefoot in the grass.

He wears shorts and
sandals, except for a
few days in the winter
when it gets cold.

AJ has never seen snow.

It never, ever snows in Florida.

AJ's mom is a meteorologist on TV. She says it's usually too warm in Florida for snow.

"Every now and then when it gets really, really cold, a few snowflakes may swirl from the sky," AJ's mom tells him, "but it won't stick to the ground or pile up high."

"Cold air comes from the North Pole," she says.

"Florida is far away from the North Pole. By the time the air gets to Florida, the sun has warmed it so much that we usually just get rain instead of snow."

AJ likes that his mom is a meteorologist.

She teaches him a lot about the weather.

"Snow is frozen water," AJ's mom tells him.

"When water droplets inside clouds are in really cold air, the water freezes and snow forms. If the air is really warm, the snow melts, and the water falls as rain."

On the news last week, AJ heard his mom say that 49 states were covered with snow.

Only one state did not have snow -- Florida!

It never, ever snows in Florida.

AJ has never built
a snowman...

or had a snowball fight with his sisters...

or had school cancelled,

because of too much snow.

AJ's cousins live in Michigan.
It snows a lot in Michigan.

AJ's cousins go ice skating outside, and ride their sleds down snow-covered hills. They wear thick winter coats and boots, and sometimes have to stay home from school because there is so much snow.

AJ has never gone to
Michigan during the winter.

His family only visits in the
summer when there is no snow.

AJ wants to play in the snow. He wants to build a snow fort, and make footprints in the snow. He wants to feel the snow on his face, and let snowflakes fall on his tongue.

But mostly AJ wants it to snow in Florida.

It never, ever snows in Florida.

It does get cold in Florida. Sometimes AJ sees frost on the grass and on his mom's car windows.

Sometimes he can see his breath when he talks. Sometimes he has to wear a warm coat and mittens to school. But when it's cold in Florida, it doesn't last long.

AJ has never seen a whole pile of snow in Florida.

It never, ever snows in Florida.

One day, AJ's mom decided to take him to the library to read about the times it has snowed in Florida.

They found stories of snowflakes falling from the Florida sky. They saw pictures of snow covering the ground in North Florida.

AJ's mom showed him that it has snowed in Florida in the past, and it may snow again in the future.

But snow in Florida is very rare.

"You can't say it NEVER snows in Florida," said AJ's mom, "because every so often it does."

So even though AJ has never seen snow in Florida,

he now knows...sometimes it DOES snow in Florida!

Made in the USA
Columbia, SC
10 October 2018